Ride On, Will Cody!

A Legend of the Pony Express

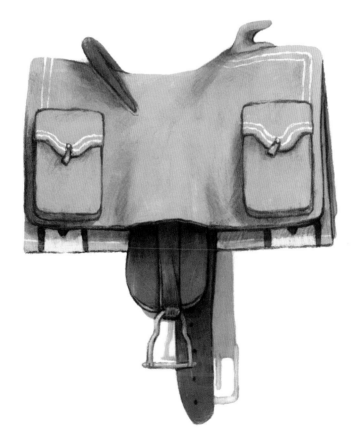

Caroline Starr Rose

pictures by
Joe Lillington

Albert Whitman & Company
Chicago, Illinois

Night surrenders,
first light embers,
fiery sunrise
way out west.

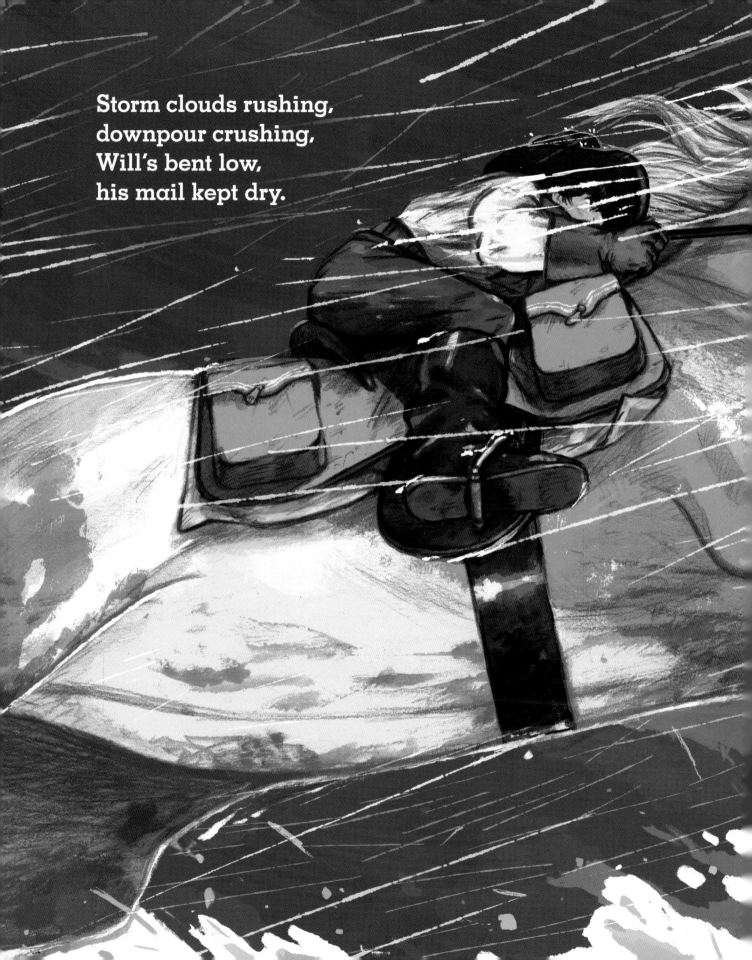

Storm clouds rushing,
downpour crushing,
Will's bent low,
his mail kept dry.

Racing, flying,
ever riding,
hurry, hurry on ahead.

Trade a Morgan for a Pinto,
Bronco for a Thoroughbred.

Lonely race,
pick up the pace!
Barrel down
the dusty plains.

Swiftly going
'cross Wyoming,
Will grips tight
his leather reins.

Horses nicker,
heart beats quicker,
saddle up
for the Pony Express.

Fleet foot glider,
wiry rider—
See them soar!
Watch them fly!

Lightning flashing,
horse hooves splashing,
station sighted
down the pass.

Seconds counting,
quick dismounting,
set to trade
his mail at last.

Workday ended,
strength expended,
Will can tell
there's something wrong.

No rider waits!
Mail can't be late!
One ragged sigh,
then Will rides on.

Falcon drifting,
rising, lifting
high above
the great bird sails.

Will sets his sights,
still full of fight—
come what may,
he will not fail.

Trade a Mustang for a Morgan,
'Loosa for a Thoroughbred.

Racing, flying,
ever riding,
hurry, hurry on ahead.

Station shines
on the horizon,
hoofbeats thunder,
echo 'round.

Fresh horse raring,
new bag bearing,
now Will Cody's
homeward bound.

Muscles aching,
thirst a-blazing,
kerchief slick
with sweat and grime—

Twenty horses,   twenty hours,

pushing on

in record time.

Gallop
faster,
short bit
farther,
last post
spotted
just up
yonder.

Don't give up,
keep steady, strong.
Mind the mailbag.
Won't be long!

Nighttime fading,
skies now graying,
dashing down
the final track.

At the station,
celebration.
What a rider!
Welcome back.

"One wild dash across the prairie—
that fearless race was legendary."

ABOUT THE PONY EXPRESS AND WILL CODY

In 1860 the quickest way to send a letter from the East Coast to California was by boat—either crossing Panama by land and continuing by sea up the western coast or by sailing around the tip of South America. Determined to provide a faster overland route for mail delivery, business partners William Hepburn Russell, Alexander Majors, and William Bradford Waddell organized the Pony Express. The service charged five dollars per half ounce (about $130 today). Riders on horseback carried mail from St. Joseph, Missouri, to Sacramento, California—a 1,966-mile route.

The work was not easy. Riders covered between seventy-five and one hundred miles per day, exchanging horses such as Pintos, Morgans, Kentucky Thoroughbreds, Appaloosas, and Mustangs (also known as Broncos) at swing stations roughly fifteen miles apart. The riders carried *mochilas*, mailbags made to fit over saddles that could hold up to twenty pounds or roughly sixty pieces of mail. Because keeping to the schedule was crucial, riders learned to dismount, swing the mochila over the saddle of the next available horse, and leave a station in seconds.

It was understood the mochila would be handed off at all costs—even if it meant death for the horse and rider. Six riders indeed lost their lives while riding for the Pony Express.

According to legend, Will Cody, later known as America's greatest showman, Buffalo Bill, rode for the Pony Express at the age of fifteen. His most famous ride, recounted in this story, required twenty-one horses. He rode for twenty-one hours and forty minutes straight: it was said to be the third longest ride in Pony Express history. By Cody's account, he started the journey at the Red Buttes station in Wyoming. When he completed his normal seventy-six-mile run at Three Crossings, Wyoming, no one was there to take the mail. He continued on eighty-five more miles to Rocky Ridge, Wyoming, where he traded mochilas and rode all the way back to Red Buttes, arriving ahead of schedule. (The actual distance between Red Buttes and Three Crossing is ninety-one miles. Continuing on to Rocky Ridge is another fifty miles, bringing the ride there and back to 282 miles—forty less than the 322 miles Cody claimed.)

Cody once described the Pony Express

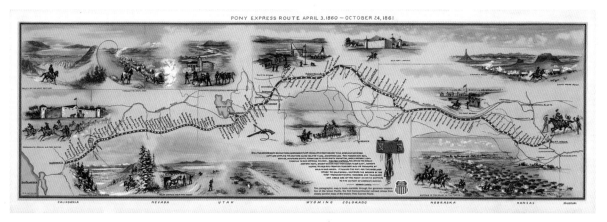

Pony Express route April 3, 1860–October 24, 1861 by WH Jackson; issued by the Union Pacific Railroad Company in commemoration of the Pony Express Centennial, April 3, 1960–October 24, 1961.

show with hundreds of actors who recreated stories of the American West for audiences around the world.

Did Will Cody really make the round-trip ride from Red Buttes? Murky facts leave historians divided. Many are convinced he never rode for the Pony Express at all. Perhaps the tale of his most famous ride was someone else's story that he claimed as his own. Or maybe, like a dime novel adventure, the story started with an element of truth but was exaggerated. One thing is certain: the short-lived Pony Express could well have been forgotten if not for "Buffalo Bill's Wild West." Audiences around the world witnessed breathless reenactments of a rider thundering into a station, swinging his mochila from one saddle to the other, and switching horses for the next leg of his journey. Through these performances, the Pony Express lived on.

as "a relay race against time" and said that "fifteen miles an hour on horseback would, in a short time, shake any man 'all to pieces.'" Imagine how he might have felt after finishing the round trip from Red Buttes to Rocky Ridge!

By October 1861 the first transcontinental telegraph line had been completed, allowing communication to flow freely across the country. There was no longer a need for the Pony Express, which ended after an eighteen-month run.

Will Cody went on to serve as a buffalo hunter for the Kansas Pacific Railroad work crew—where he earned the nickname, "Buffalo Bill"—and an army scout and guide. He also became a folk hero, as hundreds of dime novels (inexpensive, exaggerated adventure stories) were written about his life. Dime novelist Ned Buntline encouraged Cody to play himself on stage, where Cody discovered that while he wasn't a polished actor, he was a natural showman. Soon after, Cody gathered a troupe of western performers who toured together, and he eventually opened "Buffalo Bill's Wild West", an outdoor

Whether true or not, Cody's story of his ride embodies his larger-than-life persona and exemplifies the strength, determination, and courage of the young men who rode for the Pony Express—a legendary tale about an extraordinary moment in history.

William "Buffalo Bill" Cody, c. 1880

For Dan. I'm so glad we're
on this journey together.—CSR

Library of Congress Cataloging-in-Publication data is on file with the publisher.

Text copyright © 2017 by Caroline Starr Rose
Pictures copyright © 2017 by Joe Lillington
Art and photographs on pages 30–31, Library of Congress,
Prints & Photographs Division, LC-USZC6-57
Published in 2017 by Albert Whitman & Company
ISBN 978-0-8075-7068-5

Printed in China
10 9 8 7 6 5 4 3 2 1 HH 22 21 20 19 18 17

Design by Ellen Kokontis

For more information about Albert Whitman & Company,
visit our website at www.albertwhitman.com.